Pryce Gwynne

**Poems and Ballads**

Pryce Gwynne

**Poems and Ballads**

ISBN/EAN: 9783337206574

Printed in Europe, USA, Canada, Australia, Japan

Cover: Foto ©Andreas Hilbeck / pixelio.de

More available books at **www.hansebooks.com**

# POEMS AND BALLADS.

# POEMS AND BALLADS

BY

## PRYCE GWYNNE.

" Whate'er is lovely is divine."—*Burton*.

London

## T. FISHER UNWIN

MDCCCLXXXIII.

UNWIN BROTHERS, THE GRESHAM PRESS, CHILWORTH AND LONDON.

# CONTENTS.

# CONTENTS.

# THE TERRORS OF NIGHT.

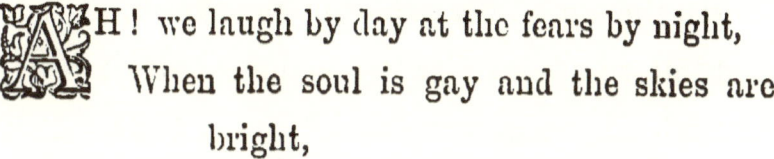

**A**H ! we laugh by day at the fears by night,
    When the soul is gay and the skies are
        bright,
Unheeding the sound of the noontide chime,
Or the rustling wings of the vampire Time ;
For only by night, in the stillness drear,
Their fluttering sounds in the wakeful ear,
Like the conchèd shell's monotonous moan,
Or the drowsy hum of the beetle's tone.
Though this in the golden noon appears
To be but the " musick of the spheres,"
But at eve—ah ! at eve—when the sun sinks down,
And the mystical gloaming buries the town,

Where the quaint old gables midway meet,
And totter and nod o'er the bouldered street ;
Ah ! why do we peer in the deepening gloom
That lurks in the nooks of the lonely room,
As the glare of the firelight faints and falls,
And the shadows steal o'er the wainscot walls,
Like thoughts o'er the brain, and lines o'er the
       brow,
When we feel they are there though we know not
       how.
Oh, what are these terrors that night conceals,
Which the mind repels, which the spirit feels—
These vague, evolving things which seem
The beings that haunt a dreadful dream ?
Say what are they, and the mystic notes
That come from the shadows' shapeless throats,
As if viewless garments were trailing o'er
The precincts of the days of yore,
Though we know not if there be really a sound,
Save the echo of heart a thought has found.
But we laugh no more, but while we muse,
We say that it is but the falling dews

As they drip from the trees so sad and still;
Or the song of the distant purling rill,
As it wanders among the dewy bells
That nod in the dreamy woodland dells.
But when from her cloudy couch the moon
Uprising steals, in her silvery shoon,
Far over the shadowy wildwood bowers,
And over the ruins' crumbling towers,
And the creeping winds awake and pass
From their haunts in the tangled river grass
And the dreary fens and the dark morass;
Oh then their uneasy, whispering moans
Evoke from our spirits responsive tones,
While the moonlit arras sways and sways
Till the armèd figures their bucklers raise,
And the eyes of the pictures draw like fate,
And follow the orbs they fascinate,
Or direct their gaze towards a ghastly bust
That gloats in a niche in a shroud of dust,
With a mocking smile in its face and eyes,
As the black-winged clouds flit over the skies,
And the expiring taper flickers and flares,

While the night suspiring wears and wears,
Hanging o'er heart and moistureless eye,
Like an ominous, dark, ill-omened sky,
Till we feel that our feet would bear us away,
But something binds them and bids us stay.
Impalsying then weird musick rolls
Through the cavernous depths of our fearful souls,
And we feel that though lonely we are not alone,
For a presence evolves from the night's dark
    throne,
Which narrows in circles, o'ercoming the will,
And weaving around us its meshes of ill,
Till our spirits, like birds, draw nearer and near
To the reptile of terror we feel and fear;
A terror which is not a vulgar dread,
But a fear the nervous never have fled,
A terror weird and ne'er defined,
Subtle and viewless as poisoned wind
That floats above some fetid sea,
Or stagnates 'neath the upas tree:
A ghastly, shapeless, nameless fear,
Evolved from regions lone and drear,

From where eternal midnight sleeps
Under the ocean's central deeps,
From where dread Lethe's turgid waves
E'er welter through the abysmal caves,
From every dark unhallowed spot
That Eblis owns and God knows not.

## LONG AGO.

I HEAR sad musick loud and long
    Upswell in every poet's song;
I see a crowd in every street
E'er seek the peace it ne'er shall greet,
Since that, with all sweet things, we know
Was lost with Eden long ago.

Free agents we whose lives begin
By being conceived and born in sin;
We cannot live free from this ill,
But, living, must the curse fulfil;
But sin and battle, this we know,
Began in heaven long ago.

Now round the heart, that living shrine,
Memorial tendrils intertwine;
The flower-like hopes that made it gay
Uneasy winds have blown away;
I prized them once, but now I know
Their loveliness was long ago.

Then give me sleep, I am athirst,
For Memory's waters are accurst.
I long for that Lethean stream
Whose waters quaffed I should not dream
Of all that was, nor wake to know
That river perished long ago.

Yet could my days be still serene,
Could I forget whate'er has been,
Or hope restore my spirit's power,
As rain revives a dying flower;
For only this I would not know,
The region men call Long Ago;

Which is where reedy grasses wave
In tufts above the lonely grave;
Where none will sigh though many pass,
Save winds that rustle through the grass;
And even they, in accents low,
Will ever whisper—Long ago.

## SONG TO PSYCHE.

GO, weary sprite, outspeed the night,
  And seek the land of dreams,
Whose cloudy light is lest the sight
  Be blinded by its streams,

That wash the walls of magic halls,
  Whose forms for ever change;
Though each enthrals the glance that falls,
  Upon its fabric strange.

There, unlike ours, the domes and towers,
  Ne'er echo sorrow's moan;
Nor are its bowers of starry flowers
  Ephemeral like our own.

For spring pervades that land of shades,
    And elfins bright and fair,
By cool cascades within its glades,
    Bedeck their golden hair,

Or mount the skies with butterflies,
    Whose iris-tinted wings
Then gently rise to Paradise,
    Where Poetry plays and sings.

For elves are souls (whom Love controls)
    Escaped from earth but late;
Where over scrolls and rouleau rolls
    Sit envy, hope, and hate.

Then hence and meet with guerdon sweet,
    And never pale Regret;
For though so fleet she cannot beat
    Thy powerful pinions yet.

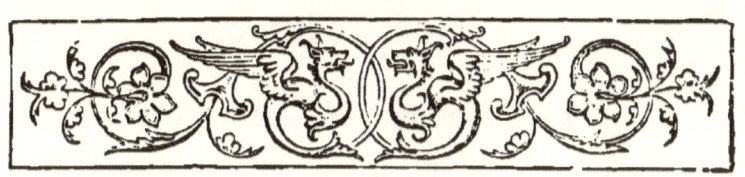

## ELEGEIA'S REQUEST.

"I feel the flowers growing over me."—KEATS.

I HAVE loved all loveliness
More than tongue could e'er express,
Surely 'twould not grant me less
    Than a lovely grave.
Little boots it where I go,
Still in life 'twere sweet to know
    The promise which I crave.


It will be the latest day
I shall trouble those who stay,
Therefore let me have my way.

Take me far from haunts of men,
Where the ferns grow green and cool,
And the stars peer in the pool,
    Lying in some wooded glen.


In a wood then let me lie,
Where the runnel ripples nigh,
And the breezes wander by
    With a dirgeful melodie.
Graven urn nor storied tomb
Shall I need within its gloom,
    Epitaph nor elogie.


Glow-worms shall be lamps for me,
Dirges chaunt the drowsy bee,
Incense rise from shrub and tree,
    Swaying gently all around ;
For a woodland draped in dew,
Where the wild-birds warbling woo,
    Holier is than holy ground.

Toll for me no iron bell ;
Water tumbling down the dell,
Echo weaving many a spell,
   Have a deeper tone and power ;
Softer than the requiem's strain
Fall the murmurs of the rain
   On the silence of that hour.

Weep not either o'er my bed ;
Nodding flowers above my head
Plenteous tears o'er me will shed.
   Never weep then, friends, for me ;
All regrets for those no more,
And the memories of yore,
   Time shall soften unto ye.

## *BEFORE THE STATUE.*

BEAUTY, art thou but a dream
    Whose wings awhile on earth are furled
Ere spreading in the brighter beam
    Of some more highly favoured world?
I know not but all men may find
    Thy shadow still in things accurst;
But if thou art, 'tis from the mind
    Of Him above who dreamt thee first.
Before thy statue standing here,
    Oh, how I tremble!  Tired and lone
To me, as to Pygmalion dear,
    I almost wish it changed from stone;
For in its faultless form and face,

And looped and braided wavy tress,
And snowy limbs and matchless grace,
    There is unearthly loveliness :
That loveliness which is to me
    As some wild musick soft and low,
Such as the syrens chaunt at sea
    By coral reefs ere tempests blow.
Its dreamy beauty re-illumes
    My memory to Ida's groves,
Embowered amid empurpled glooms,
    The dreamland where my spirit roves.
O nereid goddess from the foam,
    Though one should paint with master hand,
As did the bards of Greece and Rome,
    Thy praises to this castled land,
Which never was a classic isle,
    Set like a gem in sparkling seas,
No region where the columned pile
    Doth moulder bowered in ancient trees;
But modern Carthage, strong and cold:
    Not colder is thy statue now.
Oh, 'twould not listen.  Schemes for gold

For ever occupy its brow.
    The classic lands that worshipped thee
It says were heathen in its pride :
    The Golden Calf it *will not* see
Is monstrous by thy statue's side.
But some there are who feel thy sway,
    Who haunt these years of garish light,
To whom thou art not day by day
    A dream to please the idle wight.
Of these some live in rush and riot,
    And some in meads of asphodel,
And some in manors dim and quiet,
    And wheresoever man may dwell.
But to the wanderer in the mist
    That aye distils a tearful dew,
Thine eyes are stars of amethyst,
    The beacons of the distant view.
Where, on each upland lawn and lea,
    Made musical by sinuous rills,
The moly and anemone
    Are blooming for unconquered wills.
To only these Renown shall give

The wreath of amaranthine flower,
And only those by death shall live
  Who wield the shadow of thy power.
Then help me, goddess, help me now ;
  Before me stands thy statue lone,
And to its loveliness I bow :
  To thee—to Beauty, not to stone.

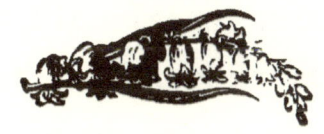

## A DREAM OF ENDYMION.

IN my chamber, when Maytime was over,
　　I sat gazing out at the sky,
And the wolds of the sweet-scented clover,
　　And furrows of upshooting rye.
All around me lay books in confusion,
　　The shrubberies swayed in the wind,
And night seemed a lovely illusion,
　　Which suited my tenor of mind.

Thus I gazed at the mystical number
　　When spirits have power o'er the soul,
Till I passed by the portals of slumber,
　　Aweary of reason's control,

To a region of shadows and stories,
    Outstretching from heaven to hell,
Where the glooms are increased by the glories,
    Which nothing of earth can excel.


Through the day I had studiously pondered
    O'er astral and planetry powers;
Now methought upon Latmos I wandered
    Through beds of somniferous flowers,
Which upsprang all around me in legions,
    Exhaling a dreamy delight,
While afar in the heavenly regions
    The stars glimmered faintly in sight.


There I roamed when I chanced to discover
    A pallid but beautiful form,
" 'Tis a statue (I said) of a lover,
    O'erturned by the wind in a storm."
But that moment dim radiance slanted
    Between the dark boughs of a tree,
And I thought now this place is enchanted,
    For what may these mysteries be.

Then the beaming grew brighter and nearer,
  Discovering shadowy sheep,
And the statue grew human and clearer,
  And seemed but a shepherd asleep.
And through vineyard and clustering coppice
  The musical rivulets ran,
And the lethargic winds in the poppies
  Intoned then a pæan to Pan.


While a sphere from the eastward upstealing
  Emerged in a halo of beams,
To all Sabian watchers revealing
  The beautiful planet of dreams;
And the labouring breast of the sleeper,
  Upheaved with a tumult of sighs,
And the pallor of Saturn grew deeper,
  The stars were withdrawn from the skies.


So, bewitched by its beauty, yet fearing
  The magic it breathed o'er the place,
I determined its hour of appearing.
  Its aspect proved love in its face,

Thus I knew why the dreamer was shaken,
   As leaves which the rain trickles through.
Ah! why did I ever awaken
   To doubt if the vision were true ?

Then adown from that silvery aidenn,
   Extinguishing heaven above,
In a mist came a beautiful maiden,
   The goddess of Beauty and Love,
And inwound him about with her tresses,
   Unloosed by the speed of her flight,
Till the poppies, who saw their caresses,
   With passion grew pallid and white.

But now, as I watched them in wonder,
   I envied the shepherd at heart,
Till he faded and melted asunder,
   As vapours that dwindle and part,
As night, when the day doth supplant her,
   Is merged in the solary beams ;
Yet I knew not the wizard enchanter
   Was Morpheus, the spirit of dreams.

Then a magical influence o'er me
  Discovered the change I desired,
And I sighed to the spirit before me
  The passion her beauty inspired,
As I whispered her, " Let us not sever,
  I offer thee labour and life,
Let me soar to thy planet and never
  Revisit this region of strife."


Then she answered me softly, " O mortal,
  For one yet encumbered with breath,
Thou hast passed by the uttermost portal
  Ere reaching the barrier Death ;
Still, to ramble within my dominions,
  The waters of Styx thou must brave ;
No mortal has e'er spread a pinion
  That crossed not that terrible wave."


Said I then, " O beautiful Venus,
  I'll build thee a palace of flowers ;
Stay here, and no shadow between us
  Shall darken these starlitten hours."

But she answered, " The planets are waning,
   And yonder is Mercury's ray,
And the sign of the spectre remaining,
   Betokens the end of my stay."

As she said it her murmurs grew weaker,
   Then melted away in a sigh,
And I felt that the beautiful speaker
   Was soaring afar in the sky.
And awaking I saw the Night's daughter
   Receding all pale o'er the lea,
While afar, in the opposite quarter,
   The sun rose aflame from the sea.

Ah, the envious, jealous Aurora
   Had whispered to Mars of our bliss,
Who sent then his messenger for her
   To beckon her up from my kiss,
To her home in the lunary mountains,
   Whose silvery summits uprear
From the beds of the scopulous fountains
   That cover that volcanic sphere.

But I dream every day of her beauty
    Though dwelling in cities of men ;
For I deem it, ah, more than a duty,
    To worship the beautiful then.
And at night, from her regions immortal,
    She drapes me in silvery beams,
Till I pass by a somnolent portal,
    And then she revisits my dreams.

## SONG TO ALICE HAMILTON.

WHEREFORE meet me sighing, only,
  Darkness cannot mate with light;
Why, then, like Nyctanthus lonely,
  Breathe your spirit unto night?

Fly, yes fly, 'tis Folly's fashion;
  Let me hence; I know not love;
Tempt not thus with flowers of passion,
  Burning as the stars above.

Spare, oh spare me, cruel blisses,
  Joy to-day to-morrow dies;
Prove me not with thrilling kisses,
  For I tremble at your sighs.

Look not thus nor say you love me;
　　Hush that music of your lips;
Veil those orbs like stars above me,
　　Touch me not with finger-tips.


Oh, but hide your bosom's glancing;
　　Girl, unwind your snowy arms;
Do be less, ah! less, entrancing,
　　Ere I fall before your charms.


Ha! too late! my heart is rifled;
　　Your enchantments prove too strong;
Resolution's maimed and stifled;
　　Tempstress, you have done me wrong.


Now, alas! what use were scorning?
　　Soon through coldness love would show,
As do lavas without warning
　　From the craters draped in snow.

Prudence—I no longer miss it ;
　　Scornful mouth, be yours the blame,
Curving now the while I kiss it,
　　I the frigid priest of Fame.


Yes, I feel the fire that thrills you,
　　Sweet as purple spicèd wine ;
Oh, then, love me now love wills you ;
　　Turn, oh ! turn, your lips to mine.


Turn, I cannot make resistance ;
　　Now I crave for your caress ;
Love is such a new existence,
　　Pleasure leaps where'er you press.


'Tis, oh ! 'tis, your beauty's doing
　　But who would, who could refrain ?
Love's reward is worth the ruing,
　　Tempt me once, but once again.

Then, like dew upon the roses,
   I may slumber on your breast :
Dreaming that my soul reposes
   In the gardens of the blest.

## ONCE UPON A TIME.

YES, once upon a time of grace,
　　When magic dwelt in moony light,
The queen of all the fairy race
　　Bewitched my heart in playful spite
　　Whilst roaming in the glens by night.


How sweetly then she seemed to pass
　　And dance, bedraped in lunar beams,
Among the flowers that gemmed the grass,
　　The flowers that murmured in their dreams
　　Beside the cloudy falls and streams,

As if her beauty raised a thrill
　　Of joy throughout their pensile stems,
And shook their souls with music till
　　The dews o'erflowed in crystal gems
　　From out their fragrant diadems.

Thus my soul shook beneath her spell,
　　Save which there was no joy to me,
No softer secret in the shell,
　　Nor wilder music in the sea,
　　Or loveliness on earth to be.

But that, alas! was long ago;
　　Now all is changed in every glen;
The sorrow that now haunts me so,
　　That fiend which time creates for men,
　　I knew not was Love's shadow then.

## HYMN TO POETRY.

SPIRIT of all beauty, aroma of all thought,
 Monitor of duty, never found though sought,
Light o'er shadow falling at the evening's close,
Merle and mavis calling ere they seek repose,
Butterflies that wander (fairies dædal steeds)
O'er the flowers that ponder nodding in the meads,
Light of flashing fountains in the groves of Ind,
Cavern-threaded mountains haunted by the wind,
Seas the sun forsakes not, boundless lands of
    wood,
Joy remembrance shakes not, all that's grand and
    good,

Thou hast power to measure ; even things of ill
Thou canst turn to pleasure if it be thy will.
As a lovely islet cheers a lonely sea,
As the hidden vi'let scents the fallow lea,
As the starry spirits light the sunless skies,
As sweet Beauty's merits comfort weary eyes,
So thy sweet dominion gladdens darkened hours,
Cupid's brightest pinion vies not with thy flowers ;
Earthly musick blending harsh and empty seems
To the wild transcending musick heard in dreams ;
Musick thou hast fashioned in the poet's mind,
Mystic and impassioned as the wandering wind.
Ah, if we could ever half thy beauty see,
Spirit earth could never steel a heart to thee ;
But thy form were blinding to our eyes displayed,
Seeking, seldom finding, we pursue thy shade.

## THE GLOAMING HOUR.

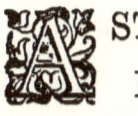 STEALTHY, soothing, drowsy power
    Pervades the dewy gloaming hour.
The ghostly breezes haunt the room,
The curtains rustle in the gloom ;
Embathed in deep uncertain lights,
The statues grow like living wights ;
The roses loll, the mellow notes
Of throstles die within their throats,
And heavily the perfume lies
Upon the purple underskies.
The earth is hushed, we must be still
The while this power o'ercomes the *will.*
It comes—it comes with force intense

Mysteriously o'er every sense,
To weave its spells and woo and win,
With dreamy bells of cadence thin,
Which peal within the listening ears
The curfews of the fairy spheres.
It comes, while on from shelf to shelf,
Evolving ever from itself;
A dusky presence glooms the air,
And lurketh vaguely everywhere.
It comes with all the soul may feel,
And tremble to, but ne'er reveal
Such as we feel when waters slip
And glide and trip, and drop and drip,
Adown and down mid ferns that wave
Within some cool fantastic cave.
It comes to cloud the reasoning brain,
Whose ceaseless logic turns to pain,
And draw the veil from histories,
That seem at noon but mysteries,
When gazing with a careless eye
Upon the deep cerulean sky;
The mote-like creatures in our view

We idly deem to fancy due :
We deem that nature has no boon
More potent than a summer noon ;
But oh, when slumber o'er us flings
The shadow only of its wings,
And midway weary nature seems
Between the realms of thought and dreams—
We feel—we feel the mystic might
That haunts this hour 'twixt dark and light,
And in these mote-like creatures trace
The presence of the airy race.
So not for aught that noon could mete
Would we, then, quit our quiet retreat,
Nor break the poppied soothing charm
Of our ecstatic state of calm,
As sweet as moonlit lakes and leas
That gleam thro' frail acacia trees.
It is not life, it is not sleep ;
It is not death, since none then weep ;
It is the sweet untainted joy
Of spirit free from its alloy ;
It is the passion of the hour,

The beauty haunting brake and bower,
The while the disembodied soul
Escapes and soars from sin's control—
Up, up, and up with dreamy might,
Through swooning shadows of the night.

# A DAMNED WORLD.

"In my Father's house are many mansions, if it were not so I would have told you."—JOHN xiv. 2.

LOOK now through this wond'rous glass ere
the hour of twelve shall pass,
For a spectrum doth arise, visible to inner
eyes.
'Tis, oh! 'tis, a sunless world, rolling through that
nether space,
Where no comet e'er is hurled but which shapeless
monsters trace,
Ever changing to reform, like the vapours in a
storm.

Aye, but see! that world is bright, fountains
    cleave its skies with light,
Like red lavas, lo, they bound spirally from mazy
    bowers,
While the cloud-falls without sound roll through
    deep ravines of flowers,
    From a soaring mountain's crown till they eddy
        down and down
    Into gulfs so vague and deep that they terminate
        in sleep.


'Tis a world as strange as fair, ne'er a storm-
    wind thunders there ;
But so faintly breezes blow round its wolds and
    valleys low,
That the banners ne'er unfurl o'er its stately-
    columned halls,
But around them vapours curl, while the dew so
    lightly falls
    That it seems but chains of gems garlanding
        the tulip stems.

'Tis a world as sweet as strange, yet the wingèd
    people range
Over mountains, seas, and dales with unending,
    weary quest ;
But no region e'er avails to afford them any rest.
    Yawning pits still seem to be under them
    where'er they flee ;
    Nothing there can make them feel anything save
    pain is real.


Say what worlds can ever roll free from sorrow's
    ill control.
Now the fiend hath set this sign in the universe
    divine,
Every wind that fans the sky, every dew-drop of
    that sphere,
Is engendered by a sigh and the falling of a tear:
    Every soul that enters there dies to all things
    save despair.

Gazing through this wondrous glass, thus I see
    that planet pass,
Rolling through a region dread, far beyond the
    night and day,
Which the stars in terror fled in the ages passed
    away,
When a curse upon it fell and that world became
    a hell,
Poisoning the upper skies even unto Paradise.

# PICTURES PAST AND PRESENT.

" Le crespe chiome d' or puro lucente,
    E 'l lampeggiar dell' angelico riso;
  Che solean far in terra un paradiso;
    Poca polvere son che nulla sente."—PETRARCH.

'EN as the cool and limpid stream
    Reflects the skies above,
So once of yore a sleepless dream
    Reflected scenes I love.


Around me, then, the valley lay,
    Bedecked by bud and bell,
And not a shadow night or day
    Athwart my pathway fell.

But far ahead the country smiled
　　With more than earthly light,
And phantasy my soul beguiled
　　With dreams too wild to write.


Then Love allured me through her halls,
　　Imbued by Beauty's power,
Begirt by woods and waterfalls,
　　And many a fragrant flower.


While ever in the evening skies
　　Uprose a double star,
Which seemed a symbol to the eyes
　　That worshipped it afar.


But dreaming now, I gaze aghast
　　Through twilights made by tears
Upon a landscape, and the last
　　Of all the coming years.

Around me now the vales I view,
   But blight is on the flowers ;
And tearful drops descend, not dew,
   Upon the dying bowers.

While Love's sweet halls in ruins lie,
   Beneath the seas of Time ;
And if my soul with Fancy fly,
   'Tis to some dismal clime.

An ignis fatuus gleams at night
   To cheer the future's glooms,
But never now the inner light
   Of hope my heart illumes.

Before me life's a plain of sand,
   The past's a flood behind ;
I seek in vain that miraged land
   No traveller yet did find.

# THE TOKEN TO E. E. E.

ALTHOUGH by this token
    I know, to my pain,
That no more the vows spoken
    Our hearts shall enchain;
Yet my thoughts will for ever
    Revert unto thee,
As the tide in a river
    Reflows to the sea;
For a thing in existence
    Is once and for aye,
It will fade at a distance,
    But ne'er pass away.
Thus in mind my devotion
    Alonely now dwells,

As the murmurs of ocean
   Remain in its shells.
But in mind, though it slumbers,
   It weighs on my soul,
As the *night*-dew encumbers
   The flowers on the knoll.
Ah, my heart is a zitter,
   This pledge is the bow;
But the tones they are bitter,
   And sound but of woe :
Like the tone that outringeth
   By Orpheus' tomb,
Where Philomel singeth
   A dirge for his doom.
For I feel as I ponder
   O'er love's vanished hours,
As we feel when we wander
   'Mid dead summer flowers.
But adieu, fickle rover,
   Go, roam like the bee,
Nor waste a thought over
   My sorrow and me.

That my faith thou hast shaken
    In love I regret,
Not that I'm forsaken
    And cannot forget ;
For my thoughts may for ever
    Revert unto thee,
But my heart it must never
    Regret that it's free.

# A MIDSUMMER NIGHT.

MOST lovely is the mystic sphere
　　Of this midsummer night,
　Dost thou not feel it, Lalla dear,
　With tremors of delight ?
Dost thou not feel that Nature seems
　All woven clouds of shade,
A land of loveliness and dreams
　To which our souls have strayed ?

So silent is the solitude,
　So lone the loneliness,
So weirdly wild yon forest rude,
　So sweet this dim recess,

That all around allures and thralls
    Like some mysterious sweven,*
That stretches out with fells and falls
    And merges Earth with Heaven.

The landscape bathes, where'er we gaze,
    In subtle tints and shades,
That mellow in the moony haze
    Of deep voluptuous glades,
Where canopies of arching bowers
    Half hide and half reveal
Their breathing banks of languid flowers
    Whose loveliness we feel.

Say, is not this enchanted ground ?
    None sweeter is I wis !
The very odours breathe around
    A soft delirious bliss.
Not e'en the angels up above
    Have dreamed a sweeter dell
In which to whisper of their love
    Than this wherein we dwell.

        * Obsolete word for " dream."

Ah, what shall test the witching rest
    And passion of this hour,
That speaks in musick to the breast
    That trembles to its power?
The softest sound in bush or tree
    That dreams on bank and knoll,
Floods far, far more sonorously
    Than thunder through the soul.

Lo where the brooding shadows swoon
    And blend and palpitate,
The ferns are drawing down the moon
    Like snakes that fascinate.
See 'how they mingle with her hair
    And breathe upon her face.
But let us go, the vapours there
    Are spreading to this place.

Come in, come in, then, Lalla sweet,
    I fear the Naiad's breath;
For when a sprite and mortal meet
    It means that mortal's death.

Her icy robes will chill thy veins,
    I feel them round me twine ;
Oh ! hasten, hasten, ere she gains
    The life so linked to mine.

## TERRA POETARUM.

" I send you here a sort of allegory, for you will understand it."

TENNYSON.

ONCE I sailed, in the prime of my happiest
time,
  O'er an ocean unclouded by care,
Till my bark touched the strand of a dream-
haunted land,
  And so I went wandering there.


All the things that there grew were enchanting to
view,
  With them nothing of earth could compare,
So that morning and night in my childish delight
  I sailed and went wandering there,

Far away in the shade, where the cataracts made
　　Ne'er a sound on the slumbering air,
Through the shadowy bowers of aërial flowers
　　Ever blooming for wanderers there.


Then I met the strange race who inhabit the place,
　　And in sorrow they bade me beware;
But the perfume intense of the flowers conquered
　　　sense,
　　And again I went wandering there.


Yet the right to remain I could never obtain,
　　For the terms were but hard, looking fair.
Few, oh, few, may abide where those spirits reside,
　　Though many go wandering there.


But, allured night and day, I went sailing away
　　O'er an ocean as dark as despair,
Till I ran with a shock on a treacherous rock,
　　In my haste to go wandering there.

Now I dream evermore of that beautiful shore,
    Yet I warn you, my friends, have a care ;
For the shell-spangled sand of that dream-haunted
    land
    Barely covers the skeletons there.

# THE TRYST IN THE DELL.

'TWAS in an isle volcanic
  Where poison blossoms blow,*
Where earthquakes scatter panic
  And woods of upas grow;
Where torrents feebly grumble
  In chasms dark and deep,
Wherein they roaring tumble,
  And tumbling fall asleep.

There in a dell all lonely
  Beside a small lagoon,
Whose banks seemed haunted only
  By shadows and the moon;

* Rafileria Patma. In Java and Borneo, &c., there are flowers three feet across, pretty to the eye, but putrid to the smell.

I once stood (partly dreaming)
　　Beneath an amber tree,
While Bula * sweetly beaming
　　Peered through its leaves at me.

But neither tree nor planet,
　　Nor creepers swayed by wind,
Nor torrents that outran it,
　　Nor anything defined ;
Oh ! not the chaos round me
　　Of gorgeous, starry flowers,
Had lured me there and bound me
　　Within those lovely bowers.

It was a something hidden
　　Upon that island shore,
Whose influence unbidden
　　O'ercame me more and more ;
For years, awake or sleeping,
　　My soul had felt its spell,
E'er urge me into keeping
　　A tryst within that dell.

　　　* Malay for " moon."

"Truth is more strange than fiction,"
    I said, half fearful still,
Though with a firm conviction
    That will had power o'er will.
"What if some kindred nature
    By love's mesmeric might:
Ah! what, if some sweet creature
    Has lured me here to-night."

Thus mused I there in wonder,
    In wonder blent with fear,
When climbing creepers under
    Some footstep rustled near;
Methought a pard's, and started,
    When, oh! to my delight,
The flowers were gently parted
    By arms and shoulders white.

The night was odour-laden,
    It seemed a lovely dream,
As through the flowers a maiden
    Then passed me like a beam,

And, beck'ning me to follow,
  Retreated through the bowers,
Her laughter ringing hollow
  'Neath roofs of climbing flowers.

" Thou art the will, the beauty,
  That's haunted me for years,
That's drawn me from my duty,
  That's caused me many tears;
Then wherefore, wherefore, fly me
  (I cried) O maiden mine?
No longer now deny me,
  My fate is linked to thine."

Her laughter rang out colder
  From out the heavy bloom,
Before me arm and shoulder
  E'er glimmered in the gloom;
And still her backward glancing
  Enticed me ever on,
Through glades yet more entrancing,
  Where gleams of moonlight shone.

And then through woods more dreary,
    More rugged and rock-bound,
'Till, growing grieved and weary,
    I sank upon the ground;
When, pausing there before me,
    She sighed, and sweetly said,
" Come, loved one, I implore thee!
    To prove thy love I fled.

" Come where the flowers are sweeter
    I wait thee, loved one, here."
And so I rose to greet her
    Within that woodland drear;
Still drearer, ever drearer,
    With every step I took,
While lovelier and clearer
    Aye grew that maiden's look.

Amongst the bushes swaying
    She stood all flushed and warm,
Her robes deranged displaying
    A bust of faultless form;

A bust that palpitated
    With passions burning free,
The while her eyes dilated,
    Ah ! most mysteriously.


I felt my spirit dwindle
    Beneath their burning might,
And still they seemed to kindle
    And wax more large and bright ;
They drew me with that feeling
    With which the cobra draws
A bird around it wheeling
    Within its fetid jaws.


I felt their magnetism
    With aye increasing dread,
Down into some abysm
    I seemed about to tread ;
I moved, a thing mechanic,
    A puppet swayed at will,
Drawn by a power galvanic,
    A mystic power of ill.

5

With fear I recollected
    That when the will gives way,
To wills by God rejected,
    The stronger grows their sway;
That unto faith is granted
    The power to move a tree,
And have its roots transplanted
    Within the topaz sea.


Thus, if this lovely stranger
    Had birth from my desire,
She'd lure me into danger
    With love's voluptuous fire;
And if she were so fashioned,
    Her beauty would control
And lure a heart impassioned
    To death to gain its soul.


Such reasons sped like lightning
    Athwart my darkened brain,
Like sunbeams ever brightening
    Through thunder-clouds and rain;

As pausing, fear-o'ertaken,
  I then adjured the fiend,
Who stood, all passion-shaken,
  Where blossoms round her leaned;

Who stood vibrating slowly
  Amongst the radiant flowers,
Which seemed like things unholy
  Within those gloomy bowers;
Which seemed as seemed that maiden,
  As seems the dead sea fruit,
Fair as—Al Gannat Aden!*—
  When rotten from the root.

Then said I, " Hence, O demon,
  And haunt my heart no more;
No longer now thy leman,
  I leave this cursèd shore.
Once naught on earth could sever
  The spell I deemed divine;
But now no more—oh, never!—
  My will submits to thine.

* The Garden of Eden, *vide* Koran, p. 57.

"The love that tempts with passion
　　I loathe, abhor, detest ;
Nor Creole nor Circassian
　　Could rob me now of rest."
Then peals of fiendish laughter
　　Rang loudly in my ear,
Like echoes from a rafter
　　Ring out in mansions drear.


And, starting back in terror,
　　I tripped ; and as I fell,
Lamenting much the error
　　That yielded to that spell,
Adown a gloomy alley
　　There burst upon my ken
The dark, dread upas * valley,
　　Bestrewn with bones of men.


* There is a poisoned valley strewn with the skeletons of
travellers in Java. The upas tree is supposed to be fatal to
those who sleep under it.

## THE WANDERER SPRITE.

"What? know ye not that your body is the temple of the Holy Ghost which is in you, which ye have of God, and ye are not your own?"—1 Cor. vi. 19.

LO here a mansion strange and white,
  Built by immortal hands,
Upon the earth a speck, a mite,
  Now lone and lovely stands;
And *I*, a wondrous roaming *will*,
  A dweller once of Mars,
Have come to haunt this house until
  I'm called to happier stars.

Once from red Mars' poppied plain,
  Through clouds that o'er it curled,
Still striving, aching to attain,
  I gazed upon this world,

Till from a grosser mansion there
   I came to dwell in this,
A fairy fabric frail and fair,
   But where I find not bliss.


Now through its tearful windows bright
   I gaze upon the skies,
To watch far up within the night
   The planet Venus rise.
And when this mansion shall decay
   From age, or fall by fate,
Then to that globe I'll haste away
   To some more blessed estate.


O brother spirits striving here,
   Death is more glorious birth !
Like me ye came from many a sphere
   To dwell awhile on earth ;
From world to world we rise and roam,
   Ascending as we range :
The clayey mansion is the home
   That crumbles while we change.

# ACKNOWLEDGMENT TO ——. *

WHEN o'er my path the deepening gloom
    Obscured Hope's starry ray,
And Azrael sat beside the tomb
    To wait me day by day,
Thy loveliness, whereat my soul
    Now thrills in weal and woe,
As day o'er night, upon me stole,
    And bade that darkness go.

# THE PAINTER'S PUNISHMENT.

" Thou shalt have none other gods but me."

THE trees are swaying in the night,
  The clocks chime out the hour,
 And dreamily the lunar light
  Besilvers tarn and tower,
 And softly drapes these manor walls,
 Begirt by woods and waterfalls,
  And many a leafless bower.

But ah, how dim the light is here !
  Like streams the shadows flow ;
My minions creep about in fear ;
  The silence will not go,

Save when the echoes mock my tread,
As if the garments of the dead
    Were trailing to and fro.


Here stands the dusty vacant chair,
    There lies the soundless lute,
Sleepily broods the purple air,
    And all is cold and mute.
All save within my listening ears,
And there the " musick of the spheres "
    Is sighing like a flute.


Oh, 'twas not thus in happier hours,
    When chaunted birds and bees
Among the flowers and jasmine bowers
    That scented Heaven's breeze.
Then Nature was a poetry book,
Melodious as the meandering brook,
    And life was full of ease.

I thought but of sweet Lalla's eyes
　　And dreams and joys to be ;
But not, oh ! not to Paradise
　　I bent my sinful knee.
I loved to dream but not to pray,
And burned for ever to pourtray
　　The thoughts that haunted me.

They were my heaven, and so I traced
　　Upon a canvas fine
My fancies and the features chaste
　　That beamed with love in mine ;
And every picture seemed to hint
That something more, far more, than tint
　　Pervaded each design.

Then oft we sought the woods at noon,
　　And there I sketched my themes ;
And oft, like ghosts beneath the moon,
　　We glided, lost in dreams.
And night and day, and day and night,
Our spirits mingled with delight,
　　Like two confluent streams.

But soon the golden sands were run
   From Time's recording vials,
For summer dwindled and the sun
   Forsook the garden dials ;
The red leaves fell, the mellow notes
Of night-birds died within their throats,
   The planets hinted trials.

Their warning passed unheeded on,
   For little recked I then ;
I hardly saw my love was wan,
   For hope was in my ken.
I only saw her radiant eyes,
And laughed at all the gloomy skies
   That loured above the glen.

" What care?" I said; " the rooms are warm,
   And ample my domains ; "
And smiled whene'er the wrathful storm
   Attacked the casement panes.
Not knowing the avenging sprite
Was singing in her dreams by night
   Of Heaven's happier plains.

Yet day by day she paler grew,
    Till, like a bramble rose
That slumbers, draped in moonlit dew,
    She looked in her repose.
And then, ah! then, my soul grew weak,
I dreamed of things I dare not speak,
    Things speech could not disclose.

And then the fiend my anger raised
    Against the spirit dove ;
For when in Lalla's eyes I gazed
    They seemed the stars above,
And I would wonder if I dreamed,
If earth and heaven and all but seemed,
    If God were really love.

So one night, nodding in my chair
    Her curtained couch beside,
Methought an angel stern though fair
    Came o'er the woodlands wide,
And bore away from out the room,
Far up within the starless gloom,
    My pale and sleeping bride.

Then, striving with the awful spell,
   I wakened with a shriek;
Around the amber lamp rays fell
   In many a mystic streak.
But all was hushed, so strangely still
That o'er my soul there crept a chill,
   Nor dared I move or speak.

I could but peer within the shade
   Of that all silent bed,
Whose crimson curtains softly swayed
   Around her golden head.
I felt, I knew she did not sleep,
And yet for fear I could not weep :
   There lay the soulless dead.

Alone, alone, with death so near,
   Bewitched though fain to fly,
My swelling grief o'ercome by fear.
   I heard the bitterns cry,
The crickets scritch about the hearth,
The mastiff howl upon the path,
   The hollow breezes sigh ;

Whilst damning accents seemed to say,
   Thou mad'st thy loves as God,.
Some one is dead, and now for aye
   Thine art shall be thy rod,
E'er toiling fame thou shalt not find,
But shade shall haunt thy heart and mind
   Till thou art 'neath the sod.

And I am conscious of a shade
   That dogs me like mine own,
And wheresoe'er I yet have strayed
   I ne'er have been alone;
It haunts the very things I paint,
So now my pictures bear a taint
   And every song's a moan.

Oh, whither, whither shall I fly?
   My life is overcast,
Though sleep should close my weary eye
   My soul is in the past;
I cannot hope for future bliss
Because the rod I cannot kiss,
   Say, shadow, shall this last?

The very portraits on the wall
   Are come to life again ;
The mocking armoured figures call
   Till frenzy fires my brain.
All things have eyes, most evil eyes ;
Into my soul each eyeball pries
   To see its damning stain.

I cannot shut them from my sight,
   Again hope ne'er shall be,
For down and down for aye by night
   The star-eyes glance at me ;
And from the sun I'm forced to turn,
Its rays like fever sere and burn,
   My heart's a whirling sea.

So now the trees may nod and sway,
   The clocks chime out the hour,
And Dian drop her silver ray
   O'er turret, tarn, and tower ;
But in my heart no ray can be,
No hope, no faith, in aught I see,
   Nor love's enchanting power.

Not even nature now can thrall,
　For cursed is my domain,
And so this old ancestral hall
　May heave and split in twain ;
And would it did with storm and fire !
It were a fitting funeral pyre
　To rid me of my pain.

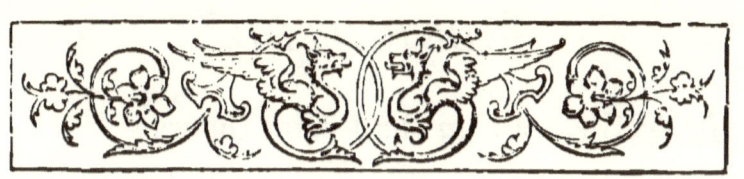

## THE PREDICTION.

THOU art aweary and would rest
  From all that is and that which seems,
From hate and love the worst and best,
The never-ending useless quest,
  And all Ambition's restless dreams.

Therefore for thee some night shall keep,
  Amid perpetual silent glooms,
A long and lasting dreamless sleep
An iron slumber dark and deep
  As that which haunts Ptolmeian tombs,

And close for aye Time's pond'rous tome
  And Life's tumultous history,
Blot from thy sight the boundless dome,
Where worlds on worlds for ever roam,
  By Death, that shoreless mystery.

6

## BENIGHTED.

N E'ER a sign shall point the way
  Through this world with danger rife ;
Such methought but yesterday
  Were but dreamy words of life,
Now I find them truthful words.

  Whither have I madly strayed ?
Chirp of grigs * and songs of birds
  Fainter grow in mead and glade ;
All around is wild and dread ;

  Pathless lies the sedgy fen ;
And below me swamps outspread
  Far beyond my furthest ken ;
Homeward wild birds swiftly hie,

    * Grasshoppers.

And upon the air by fits
Comes the weird unearthly cry
  Of the mystic lone peewits;
Brooklet murmurs wild and free
  Mingle with the beetle's hum;
Sadly moans each voiceful tree,
  For the weird-wild night is come.
Over holms, and weald, and wold
  Dark, portentous shadows steal;
Banks of changing clouds unfold
  All the blackness they conceal;
Mists hang looming o'er the mere
  Where the pallid lilies blow;
Wandering winds come not anear,
  Save with accents soft and low;
Brake and bramble clamber round,
  Oozy mosses softly creep:
Surely 'tis enchanted ground;
  Nature broods but does not sleep;
Shadow, shadow mergeth all,
  And the air is hushed and warm,
Heaven seems a funeral pall,

Earth a gloomy, lifeless form.
Ivies drape the ruined towers,
　　Mouldering in mist away ;
Death-dews sleep upon the flowers,
　　Where the sunbeams laugh by day ;
Owlets flit athwart the skies,
　　With uneasy endless quest :
Oh, these vampire butterflies
　　Are the spirits of unrest.
Dark and darker grows the night.
　　Ho ! it comes, the thunders crash !
See the curlews with afright
　　Startle at the lightning's flash ;
Fitful gusts now rise and die,
　　Bowing down the birches' tops,
While from out the baneful sky
　　Rain comes down in heavy drops.
Ha ! a glimmer in the gloom.
　　Hillo ! master, never fear.
Vainly might I shout till doom,
　　Who in such a storm could hear ?
Yes, it moves this way again.

Hillo! hi! good shepherd, haste!
Like a deluge pours the rain,
    Like a river runs the waste;
Loud and louder howls the blast,
    Deepening thunders roll and roar,
Lashing rains drive madly past,
    Lightnings show the darkness more.
Help me in my dire distress;
    Guardian spirit, help thou me;
Lead me from this wilderness,
    *Miserere domine.*

## TO ELEGEIA.

ET me look within thine eyes,
   Let me look awhile and dream,
For therein my image lies,
   Like a shadow in a stream ;
Will thy heart now ever bear
That reflection floating there ?

Though my fingers wandered o'er
   These uneasy zitter * strings,
Though with vows I should implore,
   Both at best were useless things ;
For, alas, they could not show
All that I must have thee know.

   * A sort of lute played upon the table.

Let me look the love I own,
  Lips are powerless to reveal;
Musick's most impassioned tone
  Could not breathe the love I feel;
Only through those orbs divine
Must my spirit speak to thine.


For as beams of star on star
  Penetrate the voids above,
So the spirit sees afar
  Through the eyes the depths of love;
Therefore only in their light
Can I read thy soul aright.


Let me look, then, ere we part;
  E'en as mildew kills the leaf
Woe, not years, destroys the heart;
  Love is long and parting brief;
Joyless years drag slowly on,
Smoothly, sweetly love's are gone.

And the shadow in thine eyes
　　With my form will fade away,
But the beauty which I prize
　　In my heart must ever stay,
When these words to-night may be
Nothing save a song to thee.

## *A PRELUDE.*

LADY dear, I would forget;
　　Wake not these living strings;
Remembrance only means regret,
　　And honey-bees have stings.

I cannot sing of happier years,
　　No more vain hope beguiles;
We do but hope to hide our fears,
　　We mask our grief with smiles.

For happiness, that priceless flower,
　　Was withered long ago,
When Eblis entered Eden's bower
　　To cull the weeds of woe,

Which thrive when even hope will die
    And spring from love's decay,
And stain the hands of all who try
    To pluck them from the way.


And so to smiles my lyre is mute,
    But sighs an echo find;
For sunbeams cannot play that lute
    Which trembles for the wind.


In every land, and home, and street
    Men see the shade of joy,
And follow it, but never greet
    The lovely heartless boy.


For as the moths flit o'er the flowers,
    And seek the taper's light,
Their wingèd souls in folly's bowers
    Pursue each gaudy sight.

And then they wake—ah, yes! and feel,
    When sered with inner fires,
How little in the world is real,
    How bare are most desires.


'Tis noble but to strive for good ;
    But gods of gloss and gain
Shall make the heart a gloomy wood,
    Where no sweet flowers remain.


Thus did my lips now feign a tone
    Of joy where there is none,
They'd be like Memnon's were—of stone,
    And murmur in the sun.

# SLUMBER.

YES, slumber is a heavenly shade,
 The Hermes of the throne;
To me it still hath constant stayed,
 When other friends have flown.

It cometh as a lovely sprite,
 Whose drowsy wings unfurled
Flap musically in the night
 Sweet visions o'er the world,

Which softly lie as dew on flowers
 Upon the spirit wrought,
That writhes and writhes in waking hours
 Within the hells of thought.

## THE HAMLET IN THE VALLEY.

O, is not this a lovely vale?
　　How slumbrously the roses trail,
And seem to take a crimson dye,
Chameleon-like, from out the sky,
Whose glowing orb but lately blessed
The world now sinking into rest!
Here willows weep, the brooklets creep,
The poppies nod themselves to sleep;
All flowers exhale an odorous peace;
The warbling birds their vespers cease,
And, like a dream o'er weary eyes,
The gloaming steals adown the skies,
While drowsy beetles far away,
Boom lullabies to woodlands gray,

The swaying, sombrous woods that seem
The cloudy shadows of a dream;
While around this thorp of straggling tombs,
So cloudily the vapour looms
I cannot read the stories here,
Engraved in many a vanished year.
The grasses grow in every street,
Untrodden, save by fairy feet,
That wander here in tinkling shoon,
When none are looking save the moon;
For here, then, elfin mourners pass,
Begemming with their tears the grass;
While spiders weave in many a ring
The garlands Love forgets to bring.
But now, bedraping vale and hill,
A dreamy light the air doth fill,
And all is marvellously still;
So quiet, so still, no voice nor tone
Awakes to make me feel less lone;
Naught save the low, impassioned hymn
Of water in the shrubberies dim.
Yet 'tis not strange that this is so,

For soft those bubbling waters flow ;
So softly sweet they sound, yet clear
Within each dreamer's raptured ear,
That if they could they would not wake,
No, not for even Love's sweet sake :
They long have slept, and still shall sleep
Within their couches soft and deep.
But hush ! for all is quiet and still,
Save only that Lethean rill ;
And these low airs that linger round
With voices of so sweet a sound,
Among the drooping aspen bowers
And hillocks overgrown with flowers,
Besprinkled with the tearful drops
That drip from out the willow tops,
That ever gently nod and wave
O'er many and many a sacred grave,
Nod o'er the flowers and humid grass
Whereon the footless shadows pass,
The shadows that may ne'er depart,
So like the sorrow at my heart ;
For all that's traced on yonder stone,

Is written in my spirit lone.
Too well I know this thorp and vale
Wherein the bramble roses trail.

# THE NOTHINGNESS IN EVERYTHING.

" La vie est un plancher qui couvre
L'abime de l'éternité."—GAUTIER.

IN youth we dream of pleasure,
    Beguiled by Fancy's powers,
For most have then some leisure
    To rove through rosy bowers ;
But time will soon discover
    What all men would forget,
That love forsakes the lover,
    Remembrance means regret.

Away our love is passion,
    We dream but never sleep,
Kiss lips that well can fashion
    The vows love cannot keep ;

The only joy we borrow,
   When all hath taken flight,
Is joy begot of sorrow,
   And visions from the night.


How poor, how poor such pleasure!
   How vapid is its joy!
Earth hath no single treasure
   Which will not die or cloy.
The wingèd sprites of heaven
   In joy forget our tears,
For theirs is love—ours levin,
   Entrancing while it seres.


But see yon lofty mountain
   Towering to the stars,
With cavern, crag, and fountain,
   To stop us as with bars;
E'en should one sit there lonely
   Upon that peak of fame,
He'd find the pleasure only
   A vision and a name.

Yet lashing us to motion,
  The heart's volcanic fire
Is restless as the ocean,
  For man must aye aspire.
No rest at eve or morning,
  No rest for brain or soul,
Through sorrow, scorned or scorning,
  He struggles to his goal.

So that we all endeavour
  That pinnacle to gain,
The demon whisp'ring ever,
  " Attain—attain—attain."
And if we e'er should gain it,
  E'en as he tempted God,
He'd tempt us to disdain it,
  And make our fame a rod.

To millions still he mutters
  That soft delusive *save,*
Till back the portal flutters
  Of the dark and yawning grave.

Then, near the mourners bending,
　Derisive demons pass,
Exulting in the ending
　Of life's deceptive farce.

## CAMBRIA.

I AM come to a weird and druidical region,
    Whose mountains, like Babel, to heaven
       uprise ;
Within it has wandered full many a legion,
With fanions and banners that streamed in the skies.

Then its echoes replied to the beat of their tramp-
     ing,
The clang and the clash of the falchions and mail,
The hoarse cries of captains, the neighing and
    stamping,
While the glare of the flambeaux-lit mountain and
    vale.

'Tis the land of the Cymry, Caswallon Lewellyn,
The land of my kindred who ruled it of yore,
When from high Eyri Wen* to the peak of Hel-
    vellyn †
Its minstrels related their mystical lore.


The lore of its forests and wild flashing mountains
That tumble in torrents through gorge and through
    glyn,
From the crystalline crags of the nemorous moun-
    tains,
Reflected in many a lone-lying lyn.


So if age be a proof whether races are royal,
At Saxon and Norman its people may smile ;
And who shall gainsay that a people are loyal
Who ever fought well for their prince and their
    isle ?

  * Snowden.
  † A mountain in Cumberland to which Wales once
extended.

Ah! over all Britain, unconquered, undaunted,
Its warriors fought the trained legions of Rome,
And oft as at Mona * those legions were haunted
With fear as they tore from the Britons their home.

But their goddess, great Eartha, outspreading her
    pinion,
Still kept them a nook in the land of their birth.
It is here, it is Cambria, the ancient dominion,
Whose people were said to have sprung from the
    earth.

Ah! yes, 'tis a region of gloom and of glory,
Whose beauties shall thrill every Briton with pride,
Still haunted by all its old heroes of story,
Whose voices are heard in the wind and the tide.

I hear the deep wail of their harps in the gloaming,
When cushats are silent and forests are sere,
I feel they are near me, in lone passes roaming,
And tremble to all the wild music of fear.

          * Anglesea.

Is it now but the wind or the sound of their voices,
Tho shimmer of spears or the glitter of streams,
Are those mists or the tents where proud Edward
    rejoices,
Or am I entranced by the mirage of dreams?


For round me the minstrels of Conway beshrouded,
The sprites of the caverns, the gnomes, and the
    ghouls,
Glide ever through fell and dim abyss beclouded,
And dance in the moonlight that lemes on the pools.


They glide by the rivers that trail through the
    valleys,
They flit round the walls of the legended towers,
Like the shudder of leaves in the lone forest alleys,
Their garments I hear trailing over the flowers.


Now from the jagged brow of a huge rock impending,
The shadowy waters incessantly roll;
While Dian imbues, all the night she is blending,
With beauty that wakes the wild harp of my soul.

Below me the pine tops in moonlight are glancing;
Sure Merlin enchanted these vapoury realms;
Around me in legions the red leaves are dancing,
The breezes are moaning between the wych elms.

Then awake, O my spirit, and join in this gladness,
And revel awhile where these dim woodlands reel;
For none are anear thee to call it thy madness,
Or sneer at the phrensy they never can feel.

Awake and arise and embathe in this beauty,
And sunder each fetter and bond that controls;
And worship the land of thy love and thy duty,
And pray for the peace of thy forefathers' souls.

# THE ANSWER.

H say not in earnest that Love's only
passion,
That dies in a day like the bloom of a flower,
And that none can remember or care to refashion
In fancy the sorrows and joys of an hour,
Or weave into music the spells of their power.

For though the distractions of life may awaken
Distrust and regret and contempt for all themes,
Yet over the past, though deceived and forsaken,
We rapturously ponder o'er days of our dreams,
Swept further for ever on mutable streams.

And, believe me, the heart, like a ship on the ocean,
May truly be steered and yet sink in the wave ;
And thus, though we love with the wildest emotion,
Our hearts can be lost in the years that they brave,
For time oft recovers the love that it gave.

The pinions of passion soon weary of plying,
But love is to-day a delight as of yore,
And sweet as the cadence of nightingales dying
In melody over the meadows and moor,
With the ripple of waters caressing the shore.

And all lights but this light are transient flashes
That feed on themselves with a feverish fire ;
But love, like a phœnix re-risen from ashes,
Outlives its cremation and every desire
Of pleasures that dazzle us only to tire.

Ah, yes, 'tis the passion with infinite pities !
The link of creation, the child of the sun !
The star of Ambition, the pulse of the cities
The secret of losses and all that is won !
The climax of genius, and all it has done !

# FAR AWAY.

" C'est à vous, mon esprit, à qui je veux parler."—BOILEAU.

NOW let us stray,
Oh, far away,
By the banks of the creeping tide,
O'er the upland wold
Where the fleecy fold
Climbs on its sloping side.

Away from men
To the woodland glen,
And far from our hated selves,
To look at the flowers
And the ferny bowers,
And the foot-worn rings of the elves.

There the burly bee,
Musically free,
Hums in his drowsy flight;
And the zephyr grieves
In the forest leaves
That shake in the gloaming light.


While far o'er the hill
The murmuring rill
Its mystic secret tells,
And blends with each note
Of the faint remote
Village vesper bells.


Then all around
Will be fairy ground,
And whisp'ring voices call,
Till a power intense
O'ercomes the sense,
And holds us sweetly thrall.

While the stars arise
In the darkening skies,
And glimmer one by one,
Like the minstrel's rhymes
In the gloomy times
When his race has just begun,


Our heart will cool
By the woodland pool,
And the fiends away will flee
From reason's throne,
And leave us lone,
Sweet Psyche, you and me.


It will be sweet
To escape the heat
And toil of the garish day;
But sweeter than aught,
To fly from thought
And be childlike if we may.

## CANZONET.

OH, cherish love!
  Its halcyon hours are far and few.
    'Tis from above;
  To life as to the flower is dew;
  And sweeter thing man never knew.


    But, like the flowers,
  It buds and blossoms rare and sweet
    In joyous hours,
  That speed on pinions far too fleet
  For love and time to ever meet.

For all things fly,
E'en while we cherish them, and know
That all must die
Which breathes and blossoms here below,
And that the fair are first to go.

Ah, well-a-day!
We would not linger here alone,
But pass away
When all that's dearest here has flown—
So like some lives are to our own.

Yet to the tomb
We must our best beloved bear ;
Though flowers but bloom
The while their kindred flowers are fair,
And never know grief's dark despair.

So will the years :
For grief and life are e'er the same,
Perennial tears
Drop o'er the dust that once had name :
For love and death inseparate came.

## HOPE AND FEAR.

ONWARD o'er the tide of time,
    Wearied pinions plying,
Speeding to the shadow clime,
    Hope and Fear are flying—
With the manes of recent years
Loosely draped in dripping tears.

Hope is bright and fair of form,
    Fear is dark and dread ;
Fays begot of sun and storm,
    Lovers yet unwed :
Both are gone, I am alone
With a heart that's turned to stone.

Stay! within the future far
　Hope I see again,
Stealing like a rising star
　O'er its dreary main;
While against its brightening skies,
Like a cloud, Fear looming lies.

## POETA NASCITUR NON FIT.

" Such melody was his and ready skill,
  To frame sweet verse and chaunt it to his lyre."

THEOCRITUS.

NCE there lived a bard who sang
    With mellifluous tongue
To his harp, whose magic twang
    Enchanted old and young;
Till they asked what it could be
Whose strains came o'er the sea,
From the land of Italy,
    To which he fondly clung.

Legend said it was a lute
    Which none might buy nor find;
But the answer did not suit,
    So they said it was his mind;

Though the critics years before,
Ere he left his native shore,
Said he knew not how to soar,
 And his songs were empty wind.

Other bards had lutes as well,
 Which had echoed loud and long,
Yet they paused beneath the spell
 Of his wild and wondrous song.
But the doubting scholars tried,
And they copied him beside,
Till all men were satisfied
 That their best attempts were wrong.

But his song's electric fire
 Flooded city, thorp, and glen,
For the music of his lyre
 Echoed in the hearts of men
Like the thunder-storms on high,
When they roar and roll and die
In the peaks that touch the sky,
 Far beyond the wand'rers ken;

Like the plaintive winds that wail
    Through a weary night of woe,
When the brow is damp and pale
    From the thoughts that haunt it so,
From the hidden burning smart
In the anguish-riven heart,
When beloved and loved must part
    Ere the loved one lieth low.

Ah! the deep impassioned strains
    From that lute, which was his soul,
Never sprang from works of brain,
    Which are subject to control;
For when that bard lay dead,
And the doctors cleft his head,
Nought was found—the lute had fled
    Which the nations still extol.

FINIS.

UNWIN BROTHERS, THE GRESHAM PRESS, CHILWORTH AND LONDON.

www.ingramcontent.com/pod-product-compliance
Lightning Source LLC
Chambersburg PA
CBHW032101010726
47493CB00008B/2487

* 9 7 8 3 3 3 7 2 0 6 5 7 4 *